CHAPTER ONE

THE SNOW FELL EVERYWHERE now. And the crabs kept coming.

For a while, before the grid failed and the batteries in the radio went dead, rumors hovered around that the blizzards had yet to reach a few of the tiny islands off the coast of South America, and that due to the isolation of those places, safety and warmth were still viable in this world.

But it was all theory and gossip. And even if it was accurate, what did it matter? Those lands were far too remote for us to reach, even if we could have made our way to the coast. We had neither the resources nor the skill to navigate thousands of miles of sea. I suppose there were some scattered sailors and a few wealthy folk with vessels capable of making the journey, but we fell into neither of those categories.

And besides, suppose a few islands had been spared from the cataclysm, how long until they too fell under the blanket of white and the terror that followed? Another month?

"We can't stay, Dominic. I know it's hard for you to think about leaving right now, but we saw another one last night. And where there is one, there are at least two more. And maybe this time they don't leave."

Naia is right, of course. The longer we stay on the campus, bunkered in the flimsy safety of the student union, the narrower our window of escape becomes. "It's too cold now," I reply. "Look at the thermometer." It reads four degrees.

"Do you think it's going to be in the high sixties tomorrow? In case you haven't noticed, Dom, the weather isn't trending toward spring."

I close my eyes in frustration, both at Naia's persistence and the truth of her words. "The clouds are thinning, the flakes are smaller than they were this morning. Hopefully by tomorrow it will have stopped. If the sun is shining, we'll go then."

"Sun?" Naia erupts in laughter. "The last time I saw the sun was three days ago. And that lasted what, an hour? At most?"

"Yes, but that was at sundown," I add quickly. "The sky was clear for most of that night."

Naia snickers and shakes her head unconvinced, never taking her eyes off me. "And what if it doesn't stop? What then? What if it just keeps snowing? There will be more of them. And where there is one, there are—"

"Two more, I got it."

"At least."

I hold Naia's stare for a moment and then stand. "The fire needs a log. I'll be back."

"I'll go, it's my turn."

I ignore her and walk from the dining area to the stairway that leads down to the double doors which lead out to the main quad of Warren Community College. I test the doors, just as I do every time I pass. There is a large deadbolt, but we no longer possess the key required to lock it, so the handles are threaded with a metal dog leash and a pair of thick fabric jump ropes. Whether it will be enough to keep them out when they finally decide to come, there's no real way to know.

I turn and begin to walk down the long, dark hallway that feeds into a rotunda that spokes off into various offices, as well as a large bookstore. The store has been our lifeblood to this point, stocked with a variety of things ranging from spirited pull-overs (Go Warriors!) to pocket knives. As I pass it, I notice for the first time the depletion. It looks paltry, as if picked through by wayward scavengers. We still have plenty of food in the freezer in the back of the upstairs restaurant, but the bookstore reminds me that none of it will last forever.

I move through the rotunda, down to the end of the hallway until I reach the door at the back of the building. The rear doors are identical to those in the front, except they lead out to a small clump of woods that is our fuel. I pick up the axe by the door, one salvaged from a supply closet, and grip it high on the neck.

As I stare through the lofted rectangular window, I'm entranced by the snow piling up around the base of the trees, and note that it isn't just the supplies in the store that are dwindling.

To this point, the firewood we've used to keep us alive has come from the branches of these trees, but the trunks are quickly becoming barren. Soon, the only ones that will remain will be too high to reach. Naia and I came to an agreement on the limits of our perimeter, but once the wood is gone, we'll have little choice but to breach it. Wood is everything right now. It keeps us warm, yes, but we also use it to cook the chicken, which, blessedly, stays preserved by the temperatures. Once the wood goes, and we've burned whatever there is left from within the building, we'll need to explore further into the campus.

Or beyond.

Naia and I have been alone here for five weeks. Before that, before the blast and the snows that followed, I had been a professor at Warren for seven years. Naia was in her third semester as a student, working her way up the collegiate ladder toward a four-year degree in something that was sure to be antiquated and snooty. Philosophy or art history, perhaps. Maybe literature.

Our relationship was just beginning its second month—and what was likely to be the last—when the event happened. And despite the illicitness of our relationship—and the secret we'd managed to keep from both my wife and the Warren Human Resources department—it was the affair, I know, that is the reason I'm still alive. Before Naia, any warm Sunday at noon in the beginning of May would have been spent on the back nine of the Twin Lakes Golf Club, rueing my putting stroke and shifting my focus toward the nineteenth hole, licking my lips at the anticipation of a thick iced mug and an IPA.

But after I met Naia, things changed.

I was attracted to her, of course, she's young and beautiful, but so are a quarter of all my female students. Naia though, was unique in her aggression toward me. Her pursuit, I guess you would say. She was flirty from day one, asking me questions about my childhood and my goals and political leanings. She knew of my marriage—there is a picture of my wife hanging on the wall of my office even now—but it made no difference to her. If I had had kids, which thankfully I don't, perhaps that would have backed her off. But Sharon made no difference to Naia. She pretended my wife didn't exist.

So, as our affair developed, my Sunday tee times became trysts with Naia at my place of business. It was all too easy.

Even during the school year, with the exception of a few maintenance workers and the occasional campus cop, Warren is a deserted palace, and it remains virtually unpopulated until the first cars begin to pull into the lot early Monday morning.

It was the perfect spot for romancing a young co-ed. Particularly when you have a key to the main building and a private office to carry out the deeds. It is not only convenient, it's far cheaper and less sordid than a motel.

But now the place is ours every day. There's no one else. Except for them.

The crabs.

I shake myself to the moment and unclasp one of the dog leashes and thread it through the handle until it snakes to the floor. I watch it coil at my feet before beginning on the second leash.

And then I see it.

From the edge of my vision I detect a motion through the window, beneath the snow, twenty yards or so in the distance, directly in line with the back entrance. It's not a quick or obvious motion, but it's there. A slight rise and dip of the top layer of snow.

I pause for a moment, and then begin to reverse my work, quickly re-clasping the bolt snap on the second leash as I reach to the ground for the first. My hand doesn't find it immediately, so I look away for an instant to locate it, finding it with my fingers, pulling it toward me.

I rise back up until my face is level with the door window, and as I regain my focus on the world outside, a section of the white snow is now dotted by a pair of black eyes.

The eyes are fixed on me. They blink once, then again, but never shift.

The twenty yards of distance between me and where the movement occurred just seconds ago has been cut in half. The thing is only paces away now, just beyond the door.

Despite its closeness, the head peeking up from the snow is virtually invisible. Were it not for the blackness of the thing's irises, I wouldn't see it at all.

The wood will have to wait until tomorrow.

WE CALL THEM 'CRABS' because of the way they move.

Actually though, to be more accurate, the movement is probably closer to that of a chimp or some other primate. But on that first night we saw it, just after WBXO broadcasted the military order to stay inside and off the roads, Naia saw it from the window above the quad. *A crab*, she said, and the name just stuck.

Are they dangerous? It's hard to tell.

They don't appear aggressive or hungry, and their movements are more like those of a surveyor than a predator, like they're inspecting us to make sure *we're* not dangerous. But who can really tell? A circling shark would appear that way to someone who didn't know better.

So we keep our distance, monitoring them from afar as well as we can.

They usually show up in threes, one first, followed by two more within the day. But sometimes it's more. There were seven of them staring at us from the steps of Dryden Hall less than a week ago.

A narrow ray of sun knifes through the venetian blinds and hits the top of one of the tables in the main dining area of the restaurant.

We've made our camp here, in the dining area, both for access to the kitchen and because of its second-floor vantage point. It has the added bonus of being the only area of the building with wall-to-wall carpeting, adding a few degrees of warmth to the setting.

I hold my breath and blink twice, never shifting my gaze from the sunbeam, testing my subconscious for trickery.

But the beam remains, and I stand and walk to the window, peeking back once at Naia who is still asleep in the nest of sweat clothes and fabric that is our sleeping quarters.

I scissor open my two fingers at the top of the blinds and look out at the blue sky and sun shining above. My eyes fill with tears at the sun's heat radiating through the glass. It feels medicinal. I have to steady myself on the sill to keep from buckling to the floor. I take a deep breath and smile, debating whether to wake Naia. She'll want to leave instantly, but...

I hear a sound from the ground below. It's a shuffling, wet sound, like the sound of batter being poured onto pavement.

I want to rip the venetians, but I know instinctively to keep them intact, so I pull the cord down slowly, revealing the full glory of the sun and the horror on the quad.

"Oh my god." It's Naia. I hadn't noticed her behind me as she made her way to the window.

"There must be thirty of them. Fifty maybe." My voice is a whisper, disbelieving.

"Jesus, Dominic. What are we going to do?"

I ignore the question. "Look at them. It's like they suspected we might leave when the sun came out."

"I always thought they would melt or something. I always thought the snow was their...I don't know...energy."

"Let's get away from the window."

"What are we going to do, Dom! I told you we needed to leave! This is what we get for waiting for the sun!"

I suppress the urge to argue, to tell Naia that if we had left yesterday, as night was falling along with the snow, we would have likely frozen to death in a matter of hours. And even if we had made it off campus, even if we didn't freeze and weren't attacked by the white crabs, we would have just ended up in a strip mall restaurant or the convenience store section of some abandoned gas station. Same situation, different place. How would that help us?

As if hearing my thoughts, Naia says, "There have to be people out there, Dominic. There have to be. Maybe we could have gotten to them."

This has been the elephant in the room since the day Naia and I saw the first of the white creatures hopping around in the snow. I decide not to ignore it any longer. "Don't you think they *are* the people?"

Naia looks away immediately, and I detect a look of disgust on her face. Not at the idea I have just expressed, but at me, personally, for expressing it.

"No? I'm crazy? Where did they come from then? Did they all fall with the snow?"

"Damn you." Naia's voice is low, teeth clenched. "Damn you for losing hope right now."

"I'm not losing ho—."

"You *are* losing hope! We don't know what happened. There was a blast, the world shook for a moment, and then it started to snow."

"In May," I remind with a smartass lilt.

"Yes, in May! I get it! But we don't know what happened. The broadcasts hinted at a meteor, but that was never confirmed. And maybe those things out there *did* used to be people. Maybe they're all your colleagues and my classmates and pizza delivery guys. But we don't know. And if I'm going to die from this...event...I don't want to die waiting by the last log in the kitchen of the Chicken Coop, never having made the effort to find out."

I bow my head, succumbing to Naia's feistiness. "What do you want to do, Naia? They're out there now."

"We'll make packs, supplies, enough for two days. If we're out longer than that we'll be dead anyway. We'll keep them distracted here at the front—I'll work on that plan—and then we'll head out the back door through the woods. Balmore Plaza isn't a half-mile once you make it to the clearing. I've walked it two-dozen times."

"In three feet of snow?"

"The sun's out, Dom. Let's not forget this was your plan from yesterday. 'If the sun's shining' you said, 'we'll leave then.' Well the sun's shining, cowboy, and if we don't see any of these assholes outside the back door, we're going to give it a shot."

CHAPTER TWO

NAIA AND I STARE OUT the rear door, scanning the scene for crabs while measuring our path through the woods. The blast of sunlight off the snow's crust is blinding as I look through the trees to the clearing and the shopping center just beyond.

Balmore Plaza.

With the snowfall now subsided, the storefront seems so close. Almost close enough to make it.

"I saw one out here yesterday," I say, wanting to give full disclosure about the situation we're about to put ourselves in.

"When?"

"When I went to get wood. There was one buried in the snow. I didn't see him at first, and then suddenly a pair of eyes was just staring at me. It was the same look as those ones out front. Not mean really. Just watching."

Naia closes her eyes and snickers, exhausted. "Buried beneath? Well that's not really fair."

"Do you still want to do this?"

Naia pauses. "It was just the one?"

"That's what I saw."

Naia unwinds the second dog leash around the door handles and slings it to the floor, and then buttons the top coat of her Warren College jacket. "I don't know what other choice there is."

"We could stay?" I smile.

"And do what, Dom?"

"Wait for them to leave. They always leave."

"Look Dom, if you want to stay, stay. I know you never loved me. I know you regret everything that happened between us. I know you feel guilty about not being with your wife when all this happened. You don't owe me anything."

Naia is tightening the wrists of her gloves, moving quickly through her final preparations. I can sense she's on the verge of tears and wants to leave before they start.

I don't respond to anything she's just said, mainly because it's true. Except the part about owing her. I owe her for my life.

"I'm leaving, Dom. Can you at least follow through on the distraction? I need the ones out front to stay focused on the front."

Naia's plan was this: just before we made a run for it out the back door, I was to throw something heavy through the window, the same window where we stood in disbelief and watched the crabs that had assembled below. Once the window was blown and the glass had cascaded to the ground, the crabs would be hypnotized by the whole production, and we would have a better chance of making it through the clearing to the shopping center.

It wasn't a horrible plan. Except of course if we discovered while on our run to the woods that a tunnel of these monsters had burrowed beneath the snow and were waiting for just this opportunity.

"I'll get the oven ready." I found a large Dutch oven in the kitchen supply closet, cast iron; the thing must weigh fifty pounds.

"Thank you."

"And then I'll catch up."

Naia locked eyes with me, the glisten of tears evident. "You're coming?"

I grin. "Of course I'm coming. Maybe you're right about what you said, I don't know, and I don't think now is the best time to discuss the entire nature of our relationship. But I think you're an amazing person, and I am in awe of you every day at how strong you've managed to stay throughout all of this. If I was here with anyone else I know, *anyone* other than you, I wouldn't have made it a week."

"Thank you," Naia mumbles, managing to be humble under the circumstances.

"I don't think you understand, Naia, I'm coming with you for *my* sake."

She coughs out a half-laugh, half-cry. "Pussy."

I erupt in genuine laughter at this, and begin walking back toward the stairway that leads to the dining area and the awaiting Dutch oven. It's time to go. Now. It's time to move past our false security and look for the possibility of a future, however bleak it may be.

"I love *you*, Dom."

I stop in my tracks and feel the tightening strain of my abdomen, as if snared from behind by some human magnet.

"I just want you to know that."

I nod once and continue walking.

I STARE OUT THE WINDOW down to the crabs, whose numbers seem to have dwindled slightly. This immediately raises concern. Perhaps they've spread from the front of the union to around the perimeter and are now surrounding us. On the other hand, maybe they've left for the time being, as they've done each time previously.

The crabs that remain keep staring. Watching.

The windows of the Warren student union are stained with age and the film of cigarette smoke. These are no newfangled plasti-glass windows—the kind with double layers and laminate reinforcements—this is seventies-era, junior college window technology. To look at them, they appear to be no match for the brick-like construction of the oven. One heave and the thing should blast through the panes like a cannonball through pottery.

"Are you ready, Naia?" I yell. The distance between my location and the back of the union is probably fifty yards, but in our new world of silence sound carries quite well.

"I'm ready," she says soberly. "And as soon as I hear that crash, I want to hear the sound of your footsteps running this way."

I look down on the creatures one last time, gauging the best method to send the oven to the ground. There's nothing to it, I decide. *Nothing to it but to do it.*

I lift the oven from the table and, battering ram style, swing it back once. Twice. On the second swing forward I let the thing go. As expected, it breaches the glass easily and hurtles toward the ground like a dead body.

I watch it hit the pavement dramatically, shattering like a firework across the quad, the sound deep and violent, like the crash of a mortar shell.

The plan was for me to run the instant I threw the oven, before it even hit the ground. I would then catch up to Naia, and after a few seconds of waiting—enough time for any crabs in the rear to move toward the sound—we would make our escape and head off toward the plaza. It wasn't a plan that would go down in the annals of history, but that wasn't what we were shooting for. We were just trying to give ourselves a chance.

But I was stuck in the scene, hypnotized. I couldn't leave without seeing the reaction of the things, the whole time praying they would flock to the noise like so many barracuda to a dead whale's rotting corpse. We just needed two or three minutes. It wasn't a guarantee, but it was a fighting chance.

The blown up fragments of the oven splayed at the feet of the first line of crabs, and they gave the pieces only a glance. Those behind them seemed not to notice at all. The eyes remained on me.

"Dominic, let's go!"

I step up to the open window and breathe in the cool air. The crabs had shown no interest in the weaponized oven, but my face has suddenly stirred their attention. They pack in closer, their necks still craned up at me, eyes locked as if I were a dictator on the verge of giving some nationalist speech from his palace balcony.

"Go Naia." My words are barely audible, a trial command before the real one gets unfurled. "Naia! Go! Now!"

Mercifully, there is no protest from Naia, and I hear the heavy push of the door to rear of the union. I feel guilty almost immediately, knowing Naia was expecting me to be just behind her. But I have to be sure. I have to know the crabs haven't sensed the escape happening behind me.

But they only come closer to the union, and a few of them have begun to claw their fingers up the wall, stretching their arms up the brick façade as if testing it for scalability. In mere seconds, a row of them have lined up directly below the second story window, and the next line of crabs in the party has begun to climb on top of them. They're forming a type of scaffolding and are aiming for the open window.

"Dominic! What are you doing? Let's go!"

I spin to see Naia standing on the last step. "Dammit Naia, I told you to run."

"I did. And I told you to follow me. And you didn't. So who's wrong here?"

I give one more peek down to the growing ivy of crabs working its way up the building and see they are only a row away from reaching the opening.

"Dom!"

I turn and run to the stairs, descending them three at a time and catching up to Naia at the hub of the union, just outside the campus store. The door leading to the rear of the building is open wide, wedged into a snowbank, and a path leads off to the clearing where Naia began her escape and then doubled back for me. Risking her life for me.

I love you Dom.

Maybe she does.

But I love my wife.

I wish there was some great dark secret or childhood trauma that led me to wander from Sharon, but there isn't. It was just a perfect combination of everyday things. Humdrum routine. Interest from an attractive girl. The belief that I could get away with it. Obviously, I've considered that this whole event is my punishment for the betrayal, which always reminds me to add narcissism to the pie of everyday things.

That first day, the day the world changed, within minutes after the blast when the phones still worked, I called Sharon at least fifty times. Home. Cell. Voice mail every time.

Except once.

She answered, frantically; I heard my name somewhere in the background, but it was barely a whisper on her lips. Whether it was due to the static of the connection or my wife's condition I couldn't tell. I've replayed the call in my head several times a day, every day since, hoping to find the answer, some clue that will let me know she didn't suffer.

"The snow isn't too bad. It's piled up pretty high by the door, but once you get to the clump of trees it's much lower. We can make it."

I pick up my pack, which I stored earlier beside the door, and loop my arms through the straps.

We step into the tracks of Naia's initial run, and move as quickly as we can toward the trees. Naia is just behind me.

I look back to make sure she's keeping pace, and, from the corner of my vision, I see movement through the open door of the student union we've just left. It's a wide flowing movement. Back in the hallway and steadily growing toward the door.

A steady growing movement of white.

I blink my eyes, trying to adjust my vision through the glare off the snow and the darkness of the building's interior, hoping what I'm seeing is a mirage. But there's no mistaking it. They're coming for us. Dozens of them. They've crawled through the broken window and are following us.

"Naia." I swallow, trying to compose myself. "We have to go faster."

Naia knows instantly I'm panicked. She looks back. "Oh my god."

"Come on, we can make it."

I watch in horror as the first of the crabs reaches the snow and, upon touching the white powder with its foot, assumes an animal-like pose, immediately collapsing to all fours like an ape.

Then more of the crabs hit the powder and drop into similar stances, angular and twitchy, elbows and knees splayed in preparation for sprinting.

I grab Naia's hand and run with her, slow at first as we maneuver the deeper snow, and then more quickly as the snow thins under the limbs of the tree clump.

Once under the canopy of the wooded area, we both stop with our backs still turned to the student union and the approaching horde. The grip of Naia's hand tightens as she turns around, undoubtedly with the expectation that the things would be upon us the moment she looked.

But they were still thirty or so yards back from us, creeping forward, they're advancement steady and measured, the mass of white bodies drifting outward as they approached. They appeared as a surrounding army encircling their enemy.

"Why don't they just come for us?" Naia asks.

"They seem...I don't know. Not afraid exactly...but cautious."

"Do you see how wide they're getting though? I think they're trying to close us in. Trap us."

"I see it. We have to get through the clearing before they get in front of us."

With that, Naia takes the lead into the open ground just beyond the trees. The snow is deep again, but with the sun high and beaming down, we're able to knife through it fairly easily.

We aren't fast enough to outrun the crabs if they really want to catch us, but if they keep their rate steady, at the pace we're going we can make the plaza.

I look ahead at the shopping center parking lot and the small row of stores that border it. A Thai restaurant. A diner. A barber shop. A store that looks to be a combination of craft and office supplies.

The lot is at least half-filled with cars, suggesting that several people hunkered down at the plaza following the blast.

The blast.

It had the sound of invasion. The way a jumbo jet flying just above the roof of a home sounds. Vibratory to the bone. Breath-catching. My initial thought was of war, of course. That the proverbial nukes had started flying. And notwithstanding the assurances from government mouthpieces on the radio broadcasts that this was not a military event, Naia and I still had our doubts. Especially once we ventured outside a couple days after. The landscape certainly had the look of a nuclear attack. What else could have made such a sound and then left the world a desert?

A meteor?

Yes, of course. We always held on to that as a potential theory. But it didn't fit. Any catastrophic meteor crash would have turned Naia and me to dust along with everyone else.

And then there was the mystery of the snow. I had always heard of the 'nuclear winter' that scientists hypothesized would follow a large-scale nuclear war, but I never thought the theory was literal and would involve massive snowfall. But maybe it did. Maybe this is exactly what was happening.

But did nuclear weapons explain the crabs?

I'd seen enough bad Hollywood sci-fi in my lifetime to know that radiation could turn humans into primitive white snow people. And a whole lot worse. Maybe Naia and I had great genes that were putting off the effects for a few weeks. Maybe it was just a matter of time until we both joined the ranks of this new race that was certain to inherit the earth.

We reach the pavement of the parking lot where the snow has almost completely melted. By the looks of it, the crabs have stopped coming. They've formed a broad line of bodies and have formed a type of crab barrier between us and the campus. If we don't find survivors in the plaza, the ways things are configured now, we'll never make it back to the student union. Even if we find food and shelter, there's no guarantee we'll be able to keep ourselves warm.

We reach the first of the cars and I stop, brushing the snow from the driver's side window to look inside; Naia takes a direct route toward the Thai restaurant at the far right end of the strip mall.

The car is a small sedan and looks to be empty but for a few stray wrappers and a soda can. I move past the remaining cars in the row and walk up behind a white midsized box truck double parked in front of the diner. The back door of the truck is pulled down, and an open padlock hangs impotently to the side.

I step up on the wide bumper of the truck, reach down and grab the thick handle, and heave up the door, which slides easily on its tracks.

I turn and walk inside the dark trailer, reaching the contents about halfway in.

Food. Beef and pork by the looks of it, and being kept perfectly frozen in the insulated truck. This would have been a nice treat to have back at the campus.

Behind me I hear a scramble and a click.

"Who the hell are you?" a voice asks.

I turn to see a woman, younger than me but probably not by much. She's dressed in a full coat and scarf with no hat, revealing a classically pretty face and a full head of long blond hair that's seen better days for sure. In her hands is a shotgun.

I raise my hands above my shoulders, slightly in front of me. "My name is Dominic Daniels. I'm a...was a professor at Warren."

"At Warren?" It's a shocked whisper, as if doing the calculations on how long I've been there, so close to others.

"That's right."

"We didn't think there was anyone else." The woman's voice rises at the end, hopeful, and her eyes fill with tears, unlocking a gentleness that is likely closer to her natural state than that of gun-toting protector of delivery trucks.

"There are two of us, actually. There's a woman named Naia with me. She went to see about the Thai restaurant just on the end there."

"What?" The woman's eyes turn huge and her jaws drop wide.

"The Thai restaurant. I think it's Thai. I mean the name is someth—."

"No!" she screams. The woman turns and disappears from sight, and seconds later I hear her yelling. "Hey! Get away from there!" followed by two gun blasts.

I jump down from the truck and follow in the direction of the woman, and immediately see her with her shotgun raised, and past her, in the background of my line of sight, I see three bloody crabs running away from the sound of the weapon.

On the ground in front of the restaurant, Naia's body is mangled and dismembered, the crimson rivers flowing from beneath her turn the snow to a sheet of ruby crystals.

She's dead.

CHAPTER THREE

"THEY WEREN'T LIKE THIS at first."

Tom Godfrey is the owner of the diner where I've suddenly gone from prisoner to refugee. He has a kind face, the lines and wrinkles of it show the scars of worry and weariness. He has agreed to tell me what he knows. It's been a week since I've been here, and after spending most of those seven days in a restaurant version of solitary confinement, the group has now allowed me to be amongst them.

Danielle—the woman whom I first met—brought me my meals in the cordoned off dining area which was my living quarters. She started by just dropping them and leaving, but by the fourth or fifth day, she began to linger for a word or two of superficial conversation. I never loved Naia, and it's fair to say that as the days and weeks blossomed I grew to resent her, but I'd grown so accustomed to her sole company that after three days of confinement I began to feel the symptoms of social withdrawal. Danielle noticed and threw me a bone of companionship.

"At first they just looked at us. Studied us. We stayed away from them, of course, but after a few weeks, we started getting a little more daring. Well, some of us did."

Tom's eyes drop for a moment and then flash back to me.

"My son Greg. He was the manager of this place. It's mine on paper, but Tom's Diner was Greg's in every way. He felt responsible for us. For Danielle and the other wait staff, and the customers."

I shift my eyes, studying each member of the group, trying to figure out who belongs in which category. Unlike in normal life, every one of the remaining six people in this new post-apocalyptic tribe looks to be cut from the same cloth.

"He knew we couldn't stay here forever, so he started getting a little more daring with his outings. When the snow would subside, he'd take the jeep out and patrol the streets, trying to find survivors. That's how James came to us."

Tom points at the youngest member of the group, a kid, probably still in high school.

"Did he see any of the crabs out there?"

Tom looks at me quizzical.

"Crabs. That's what Naia and I used to call them."

Tom nods. "He did. Hiding in the snows. Creeping around the fringes like they tend to do."

"Do you know what happened?" This is the big question, of course, and my choice of timing to acknowledge it is rather clumsy. But Danielle gave me no answers during our brief conversations, so Tom seems like the next best source.

"I don't. You probably know as much or more than we do. They think every place was affected. The world is over."

I bounce a somber nod. "Sorry to interrupt you. You were talking about your son."

Tom smiles weakly. "Greg wanted to see what the things wanted. The crabs as you call them. They never tried to get in, even though they could see us clearly through the glass door. That was at first before we covered it with the curtains. Anyway,

Greg got to the point that whenever he saw one he would go outside and stand there. And they would just stare at him.

Tom takes a deep breath.

"But then one day he went out and they started to approach him. He ran back in right away that first time, but then he started to...push it. He started to believe you could, I don't know, tame them, I guess, similar to the way you break a wild animal. He thought their gradual approaches just meant they were becoming more comfortable with him."

"I could see thinking that. But what was his plan? You said he felt like he needed to protect you. Like he was responsible. What did taming these things have to do with protecting you?"

"Well, if the things turned out not to be dangerous—and keep in mind, up until that point we had no reason to believe they were—then we were going to leave. We were going to try to find others. Civilization. Maybe all the radio reports were wrong and there were actually places that were unaffected. Or at least functioning. Maybe this was all going to pass. Maybe there was a cure for these...people."

"So they *are* people?" I interrupt again. I'm being a bit rude, I suppose, but I don't much care. Here are potential answers to the questions I've had for months now. "These things did used to be people?"

"Well where else would they come from?"

The question comes from Alvaro. Thirtiesh, broken English. I profile and assume he worked the kitchen of Tom's. His question reminds me of my conversation with Naia only a week ago, and I close my eyes and turn away, stung by the memory.

"Yes, Dominic," Tom answers, "they are people. The ones in Thai Palace—the ones that got to your friend when she opened the door—they were the owners of that place."

"How do you know that was them?" My tone is slightly angry now, accusatory.

Tom looks around at the rest of the group, as if asking permission to tell the story. "Their names were Gun and Kannika. Their son was Joe. I had known them since before Joe was born. Since the day they opened their restaurant over twenty years ago."

"Jesus. I'm sorry." I give a flat smile, a tacit apology for my earlier tone. "But why them? Why anyone? Why did some people...change and some didn't?"

"Only thing we can think is that it's because they were outside. When the blast happened, they were outside at the truck. They were dealing with a delivery, some problem with the shipment. A union issue or something, because the driver wouldn't physically bring anything inside the store. So Gun and Joe were stuck having to bring in their supplies themselves before the driver was scheduled to leave. The blast happened just as they began, and within the hour the sirens were sounding and the emergency broadcasts were telling people to get inside. I'm sure you remember."

"I do."

"Well Gun and Joe had work to do, and Kannika started pitching in as well. Most of our customers left, but some, like Terry and Stella here, hunkered down. Probably saved themselves. Because within two hours the snow started to fall. And that was the key. If you were out on that first day during the blast and still when the snow started, you turned into...well...that's as far as we can tell anyway."

"So you locked them in the store?" My voice sounds bitter, laced with disgust.

"Didn't lock anything. Your friend opened it just fine." Tom pauses and holds up a hand. He closes his eyes for a moment and then stares at me. "May God bless your friend's soul, Dominic. I can't tell you how sorry I am for your loss."

I give a nod of gratitude, too choked to say 'thank you.' "But how...why didn't they come out weeks ago?"

"They can't work doors, we reckon. When Gun and Kannika and Joe finished the delivery, they went in. Probably thought they would open for the day and it would be business as usual."

"Can't work doors? They can sure climb like motherfuckers." I don't bother apologizing for my language. Fuck it.

"Haven't seen that. How do you know?"

"Because the instant I broke a window in Warren's student union they started building a ladder of bodies. Like ants or something."

Tom looks at Danielle, making sure she's registered this new bit of intel. Danielle frowns and nods.

"Are there others stuck inside?"

"We think the other stores have at least one or two people inside. But most left when the warning came."

I shake my head and blink in disbelief. "Why were they so violent? The ones on the campus never appeared to get that way."

"You can't let them get close. That's the key. They're curious, but they stay their distance for the most part. They'll follow you, but they're very apprehensive." Tom pauses. "Until you get right next to them."

"What happens?" I ask, immediately appalled at my own question and Naia's fate. I tacitly retract it. "But why?"

"I don't know, Dominic. But my son was the first to prove it true. As far as I know anyway. And your friend left no doubt in my mind."

Tom lets the impact of his words resonate for a few beats.

"And we didn't mean to dehumanize you by keeping you locked behind the gate. Hope it wasn't too uncomfortable."

"It wasn't the Four Seasons, but it was fine."

Tom smiles. "We just had to be sure, you know? Sure you wasn't going to change into one of them and mean to do us harm."

"Are you sure of that now?"

Tom gives me a long stare and I'm tempted to drop my gaze, but I steel it forward. "I am," he says.

I let the power of that trusting phrase linger for a moment and then I turn to the last two remaining members of group. They've been silent thus far, but I can feel the judgement of their stares.

"How is it that you two came to be here?" I ask.

They are fortyish, a man and a woman, fit and attractive, and they sit together in a way co-workers might. They could be a couple, but it's not the sense I get.

They look at each other, and then the woman speaks up. "I'm very sorry about your friend."

"Thank you."

Naia. In my mind, I've already moved past what happened to her, despite the gruesomeness of the event. I don't see myself as a monster for feeling this way, but perhaps I should. Maybe it's because it was her idea to leave. Had I insisted we explore past the union, I imagine my guilt would run deeper. Or maybe it's some type of hyper-evolution, a mutation of my sensibilities that no longer allows me, in such an inhospitable environment as Earth itself, to wallow in sorrow at the loss of life.

I, myself, want to feel the loss more severely, and I can imagine how my lack of shock and despair must impress on the group. But I won't put on a show for the sake of decorum. I feel how I feel, and I'm moving past it.

"So? How did you two get cast in this diner catastrophe?"

The man grins. "We stopped in for a bite. Then the world went to shit."

"Stopped in? On your way to somewhere?"

"Headed to a medical conference at the University.

"You're doctors?"

"That's right. Clinical psychiatrists. My name is Terry. This is Stella."

I nod as I process the introduction, and I can feel my face scrunch quizzically. "So why'd you stay? Why didn't you leave when the blast occurred and the first news reports started?"

The woman shrugs. "Just thought we'd wait out whatever was happening. We didn't have a lot of gas, and we don't really know where we are, so we didn't want to risk getting stranded somewhere. And then the reports started to tell everyone to stay put. There was food and water here. So that's what we did."

"And what about you, Dominic?" It's Alvaro, Tom's cook/dishwasher. "Why didn't you leave?"

I frown and say, "I wish I had."

The eyes of the group stay on me, waiting for the reason.

"I was having an affair. With Naia. She was a student of mine. When everything started, I didn't know what to do. So we just stayed. I panicked, I guess. Naia thought we should leave right away, but she let me decide for us."

"You probably saved both of your lives." Stella adds.

"Probably. If we had left, gone our separate ways, we would never have made it home before the snow started."

"So why do you wish you had left?"

I pause and clear my throat, fighting away the lump developing there, and then raise my eyebrows and shrug. "I would have seen my wife one last time."

There's a long silence and then Tom says, "We've all got our sins, Dominic. But it's a new life now."

I stand. "Yeah, well, that may be, but it's not one I plan on spending the rest of in a greasy spoon. No offense, Tom."

Tom purses his lips. "What'll you do then? You leaving? Just like that?"

"Maybe not 'just like that,' but I don't plan to die here. Naia wanted to find civilization, not just another bunker to hole up in. I owe her at least the effort. But before I begin to restore the world, I'm going home."

"There's nothing out there, sir." It's James, the refugee from the snows.

"I can't believe that, son."

"I thought the same thing. After a few weeks, when my parents and brother didn't come home, I ventured out. I thought I would eventually come across something more civilized. At least something better." James shakes his head twice. "Everywhere is the same."

"I know you believe that, James, but let's be honest: you couldn't have come from very far."

"Fifty miles I'd bet."

That was farther than I would have guessed, but it still didn't quite span the planet.

"And you heard the broadcasts like we did. It didn't just happen here. It's everywhere."

"And we've driven at least that far in every direction," Danielle added. "It's desolate."

I consider James' assertion ('It didn't just happen here') and his statement about the broadcasts. We had heard them, Naia and I, first from the DJs at 99.4 WBSK, and then later, when the DJs jumped overboard to some ostensible safety boat, from the station manager. But that was it. WBSK was the only signal we could get. The rest of the dial was a low, steady sea of humming and hissing.

Where was WBSK getting its reports?

I filed the question away for later, and addressed the accumulating defeatism in the room. "So we just stay then? Until what? Until they learn to open doors and devour us? Until we run out of food and end up eating each other?"

"What's your plan then, Dominic?" It was the doctor, Terry, and the question showed no trace of dismission.

"The snows have subsided again, and seem to be coming less frequently. This box truck of yours, with the supplies, it's probably heavy enough to get around on the roads the way they are now. I say we venture out again. Tomorrow at first light. Is there gas in that thing?"

"Hasn't moved since that day of the delivery. Just been getting food from it as needed. Gun and Joe had barely gotten started on the thing."

I think back to the contents of the truck when I first arrived at the shopping center, and recall it being less than half-full. Just another reason to start planning an escape. The supplies won't last. "Has anyone tried to start it?"

The group glances at each other individually, waiting for any acknowledgement that this particular act has been attempted. No one assents.

"Okay, well, I guess the battery might be an issue, but I'd say it's a fifty-fifty shot that it will start. How about the keys?"

Danielle says, "That's probably why no one has tried it. The keys aren't in the ignition. I know that much."

"Any ideas where they might be?"

"Ideas? Sure. Probably with the driver. Don't know for sure though."

I close my eyes, knowing the answer to my question before I ask it. "Any ideas about *his* whereabouts?"

"This minute? No. But I know exactly where he was when this all started."

"Inside the Thai place, I'm guessing."

No reply.

"So then he's out now? When Naia opened the door?"

Danielle shakes me off immediately. "No, it was only Gun and Kannika and Joe that came out of the restaurant. I'm sure of it. He wasn't with them."

"So he's probably in there still."

Danielle shrugs. "We never saw him through the storefront window, as many times as we looked through it, but I would imagine he must be. Maybe he got caught in another room when he...changed... and couldn't get out."

"Or maybe he didn't change at all and they killed him," Stella adds. She looks up in thought, and then nods to Terry as if signalling him to consider the possibility.

I have a million questions about that process—the changing—and since Tom lost his son to the crabs, whoever saw that atrocity certainly has more theories about what happens. Did those who were killed by the crabs themselves become one, zombie-style? What about anyone who dies from here on out of natural causes? And why were they all naked and sexless? It was as if everything that hung loose—clothes, genitals, hair—froze solid and fell to the ground.

But now isn't the time. Now I've got to find the keys to the box truck and try to make my way home.

"So the keys are with him, then. Somewhere in the restaurant. Maybe in a pocket."

"They ain't got no pockets." Alvaro snickers as he says it, amused at my naiveté.

I give a single nod. "I noticed that. What happens to their clothes?"

"Clothes, cocks, nipples, ears. I don't know, man, it all just falls off. And then whatever's left over just closes up to white like the rest of them. You can't tell the difference between the tops of their heads and the bottoms of their asses. It's the craziest shit you ever heard of."

"Well that should make it easier. If their clothes just dissolve or something, then the keys should be on the floor somewhere. Right?" I'm trying to convince myself as much as I am the group.

"I don't know, man. I guess so."

"Why would you risk that?" It's Terry again. "Why not just go for another car?"

"And even if you do get the keys," Tom says, "I don't reckon we can just let you take the supplies. That's plenty of food in there. We can last a long time on that."

This objection was inevitable. "I can't afford getting stuck. I need the heaviest thing I can get. We can move the supplies in the truck to a few of the other cars in the lot. It will stay just as cold in the trunk of a Buick as it will in the box truck."

Danielle speaks. "Let's just see if we can find the keys first. There's no point building bridges to the next river before we've crossed this one. And besides, if we can get the truck started, I think we all should go. That's just my two cents."

The room stays silent, and I smile and blink my thanks toward Danielle. She doesn't look at me.

"Well that will be a choice to consider if we get the keys," Tom says. "But let's see about that part first. Bridges and rivers and all that."

CHAPTER FOUR

THERE ARE FOUR OF US standing on the sidewalk outside of Thai Palace. Alvaro has his forehead against the glass storefront; his hands are cupped around his eyes as he peers inside, fighting the glare, struggling to see through the gap of the curtain to the kitchen and restrooms at the back of the restaurant. Alvaro was the first volunteer to accompany me to this potential danger zone, followed by Terry and Danielle. Stella seemed willing, but Tom decided four should be the number. He made some pretense of strategy, but I think he was opposed to including both women on the mission and was afraid of being called a chauvinist. Tom is a good man. Besides, if it all goes to shit, I suppose we'll need survivors to carry on the species.

"You catching any movement in there, Alvaro?"

"I can't see shit, man. It's too bright out here."

"What about through the other window, over here?" I point to the front window on the opposite side of the door.

"You got no angle to the back from this window. All you can see is the front counter and that stupid fish tank."

"All right, we'll take it real slow then. I don't expect to find anything, but we'll take it real slow."

The restaurant has a classic knob-style door, rustic and opaque, with ornate bordering around the frame, presenting the customers with a certain old-world, oriental charm. I realize now that were the door of the free-swinging push/pull variety that most commercial establishments have, the crabs would have freed themselves long ago.

"I'll go first," Danielle offers. "I've worked in this shopping center longer than Alvaro; I've eaten here a thousand times. And you two don't know the place at all."

"What does that have to do with anything?" I retort.

"I know where the restrooms are. That's what we're all thinking, right? That the driver was in the restroom at the time."

I had thought it.

"Oh shit!" Alvaro apparently has not.

"I think that's the idea." It's Terry, and his joke gets a disapproving glare from Danielle, who then closes her eyes and shakes her head sighing.

"Okay, fine," I say, "you go first, but I'm coming too. The two of us will go in together. This is my idea, so I'm at least going to be one-A through the door. Alvaro and Terry can each take a side of the dining room and follow behind us."

Danielle gives a whatever shrug, less eager to argue than to get inside.

I turn the knob and pull the door toward me, at once anticipating both nothing and a flood of crabs to pile upon us. But there's only the musty smell of damp carpeting and grease, and of the rotting bass or carp in the fish tank framing the lobby entrance. Danielle and I pause for a moment before moving forward to let Alvaro and Terry inside. Terry eases the spring loaded door back to the jamb gently, and then we all stand stock still, listening.

"What do they eat?" Alvaro asks, a propos of nothing.

No one answers.

"I mean, if that thing got trapped in the toilet, it would die right? It couldn't live without eating."

"What do they eat when they're not trapped?" Terry asks. "We know they attack and kill, but what do they do with them. Has anyone seen them eat?"

"When I write my thesis after this whole ordeal is over," I reply, "I'll be sure to get all those details. Now, however, don't much care."

Danielle has already moved five feet ahead of us toward the kitchen. I catch up to her and motion for Terry and Alvaro to stay back a few feet and create a perimeter. As we approach the portholes of the swinging kitchen doors, the path forks sharply to the left, leading down a corridor where, undoubtedly, the bathrooms lie.

"Good thing you were leading," I tease. "I'd have never found my way."

"Just stay close."

Danielle steps down the corridor toward two doors which mirror each other on opposite sides of the wall.

"There are two doors down here. One is the bathroom—it's a unisex—and the other is some kind of employee break room or utility closet or something."

"I'll take the bathroom." I declare.

Danielle looks back at me and flashes a faint smile, showing a chip in her veneer of fearlessness, and then nods in agreement. "It's pretty tight in there and I don't hear anything, so I'm assuming if he's in there he's dead. But just be careful."

"I will. What's the story with this other room? How big?"

"I've never seen it. Like I said, it's employees only."

"Maybe we shoul—"

A scream pierces the silence of the stale air like the screech of a passing jet. I know immediately it's Alvaro.

Danielle and I backtrack down the corridor to the main dining room, reaching it in time to see the pain on Alvaro's face as he's pulled into the kitchen by a pair of ghostly white hands.

Terry comes up beside us and the three of us stand in shock, not knowing whether to pursue or retreat. Danielle decides first and bursts through the hinged doors toward her co-worker and fellow apocalyptic survivor.

"Wait!" I start to follow but stop and turn to Terry first. "What happened? Where did it come from?"

Terry remains frozen, his gaze locked on the door to the kitchen, as if waiting for the reveal of the joke that's been played.

"Hey! What happened?"

"There was a table. In front of the doors. He...he moved it and...it grabbed him."

"Let's go." I'm through the swinging doors and halfway across the kitchen when I realize Terry isn't with me. He's fled.

I continue toward the exit door at the back of the restaurant and immediately see Danielle standing tall, butcher's knife held straight and poised, staring across the stainless steel counter into an open walk-in freezer. She says nothing; she just points inside.

The crab that grabbed Alvaro, ostensibly the delivery driver with the keys to our truck, is on his haunches, staring back at us, teeth bared in a posture of protecting his kill. Alvaro is directly behind the crab, but the puddles of blood that flank him flow from wall to wall of the freezer, leaving no doubt about his fate.

"We have to go, Danielle." My voice is flat, calm, despite the flood of terror inside of me.

"We're not leaving without the keys."

"We'll find another truck. We don't even know if this truck will start. Or if that thing is our guy."

"The keys are on the floor. Right there." Danielle moves her eyes down and to the right and cocks her head in the same direction. "I guess when he turned into this thing he was standing by the freezer. And then his clothes disintegrated or whatever, and the keys ended up there. He obviously got locked in here from the dining room. My guess is that he turned just before Gun and his family, and they barricaded the door."

"You're pretty smart for a waitress."

"I'm well out of my teens, so I'm way too old for you."

I fight the urge to laugh, an impulse that's made even more difficult by Danielle's stone face and flat tone. "I'm sorry about Alvaro. He seemed like a good person."

"He wasn't really. A bit of a sleaze ball. But he didn't deserve to die." Danielle looks at me. "Where is Terry?"

"He ran. I guess he's back at the diner."

Danielle nods as if not surprised and turns back to the freezer. "Here's the plan: there's nothing to be done for Alvaro, so I'm going to move next to the counter, staring down this creepy dickless goblin while I do, which will give me an open path to the door. And at the same time you're going to move behind the freezer door. When I say so, you're going to slam the door shut as quickly as you can."

"What about the keys? It looks like they're in the path and could be swept in. Will the door clear the keys?"

"They're clear. I already calculated it. Remember about me being smart?"

I chuckle and nod, and then creep on the balls of my feet behind the freezer door, making sure not to make eye contact with the crab.

"He's fine," Danielle assures, "he's focused on me. Tell me when you're ready. Both hands on the door and push as hard as you can when I signal."

I position myself as instructed. "I'm ready. What's the signal?"

I can't see the scene as it plays out, but I hear a rattle inside the freezer and then "Now!"

I hesitate a half-second and then spring. The door is heavier than I'd estimated, and it takes me a few seconds to build up the momentum to swing it quickly.

"Go! He's coming!"

I get my shoulder into the door now, and have almost worked the large metal gate to the jamb when I feel a sickening resistance and a terrifying scream. The door bounces back toward me a bit and I heave against it again, this time getting a bit less resistance before the door finally erupts with the satisfying sound of locking in its proper place.

I push my back flat against the closed door, breathless. "What the hell just happened?"

"Not the plan I intended, but we're clear. I threw the knife inside to distract the thing, but he didn't go for it, and as soon as you started to close the door he made a run for it. You caught his body pretty good that first time and he backed off, scurried back inside. Then he made another dash on your second close, and you took a couple of his fingers off."

Danielle nods down to the floor where three white appendages lie, sterile as chalk.

"It's a good thing you got a second chance too. I misjudged the keys. If he hadn't have blocked the door that first time, they'd have gone in with him. I was able to kick them clear"

"Guess not that smart, huh?"

Danielle snickers and picks up the keys, dangling them in front of her. She smiles as the screams of agony sound from the other side of the freezer door. "But still too old for you."

"WHERE DID YOU GO?" The anger in my voice is crisp, and Tom stands and moves between me and my suspect.

Terry sits on one of the stools at the counter, his back to the door. His colleague Stella rubs his back, soothing him. "He's a bit shaken," she says.

"Shaken? Are you fucking kidding me?" I take a step toward the counter and Danielle grabs my arm, keeping me next to her. "We could have used some help. Alvaro's dead."

Tom closes his eyes and drops his head, and then sits back down at one of the dining tables. He looks defeated.

"He was dead before anyone had a chance to save him." Terry speaks without turning. "You were all dead the second the bomb hit. We all are."

"Terry!"

Stella's exclamation rings odd to me. It sounds more like a stifle than an admonishment of his pessimism.

"Maybe not." James says, a hopeful lilt in his voice. "Maybe we just haven't gone far enough, like Mr. Dominic says."

I free my arm from Danielle's grasp and move slowly toward Terry and Stella. Danielle doesn't fight me.

"What do you mean bomb? Who said anything about a bomb?"

Stella stands from the stool and walks away, not meeting anyone's eyes.

Terry looks up at me. "It was a bomb."

"How do you know that?" Danielle says, now standing beside me.

"Because we work for the people who developed it." It's Stella. She's standing in a far corner of the diner, staring out at the parking lot, a cigarette between her fingers.

"What?" James' question is a whimper.

"It was supposed to be contained. A small blast on the campus."

"What the hell are you talking about?" My fury is leaking into fear, almost despair. "Who are you?"

"We are who we said." Terry takes the reins. "We're psychiatrists. We were sent to monitor the psychological impact of a "blast event," he makes air quotes, "in a small, self-contained area. Warren College. It wasn't real. It was an experiment. It was just supposed to be a test."

"Who in God's name could have authorized such a thing?" Tom asks. "You work for the government, do you?"

"Not directly, but we're contracted by them, yes."

James has begun to cry.

"You killed my boy. Don't live another minute thinking you didn't."

Terry looks up to the ceiling as if sincerely considering this. "I suppose I played a part, sir."

"I can't believe this," I say. "I don't understand what is happening. Why would you have volunteered for this assignment?"

"It was supposed to be an experiment." Stella is almost yelling now. "Of course we wouldn't have involved ourselves had we known the turnout was this."

"So what happened?" It's Danielle, and she's steely in her tone, having moved past the hysteria. "What went wrong?"

Terry matches Danielle's demeanor. "I don't know exactly. We were never a part of the front end of the assignment. We were just supposed to observe how people reacted to the event after it happened."

"But what was the event? How was it going to look?"

"They told us we'd hear a sound. They were going to create some kind of sonic explosion in the sky above the campus. That was all, just a sound. They were going to temporarily eliminate all cell and cable service. The only information anyone was supposed to receive was from one of the local stations that they were going to commandeer."

"WBXO," I say to no one.

"So the broadcasts were fake? The ones about the world being destroyed?"

"I don't know anymore. I thought so at first. I mean, obviously something went terribly wrong—the snow and the...things out there...weren't ever part of the plan that we were told about—but I was still hopeful that this was all contained to our little area. Until we started driving. Until we found James and he told us about the distance he'd come."

Everyone stays silent for a few seconds, considering the importance of Terry's words. Fifty miles at least. In every direction. That was quite a bit more ground than the campus of Warren.

"Why would they have picked Sunday?" I say finally, shifting gears a bit. "There's no one at the college on Sunday. If they wanted to conduct this experiment on the students, why did they pick Sunday?"

"That's how we knew something was wrong. It was a day early. It was supposed to be Monday, late morning. Stella and I came a day early; we had reservations at the Marriott down the street. We stopped here for something to eat, and, well..."

"So you really don't know what those things are? The crabs?" James asks. He's regained his composure, almost resigning himself to his fate.

"We don't," Stella says, walking toward him from her corner sanctuary. Her eyes are soft, kind. "And we don't believe any of this was an accident."

"What do you mean?"

"The people we work for don't make mistakes of this magnitude. Mistakes of conscience and ethics, yes, but not the technical mistakes that would have been required in this instance."

I step away from the bar and stand in front of Stella, my face at least eight inches above hers. "So what are you saying?"

"I'm saying we're a part of this. Terry and I. We're part of the experiment."

"Or maybe you telling us you're a part of the experiment is a part of the experiment." It's Danielle, now standing next to me aligned against Stella.

Stella raises her eyebrows and nods, accepting the logic of Danielle's skepticism. "Our lives are in as much danger as yours. Or anyone's here. Do you think those things out there are also in on the whole plot?"

Danielle stares at Stella for a beat and then frowns and shakes her head.

"So all the more reason to get in this truck and leave," I say. "If this isn't the global catastrophe we thought it was. If it's just this county, or even the whole state, then we just have to keep going. We just need to find the line that divides us and the perimeter of the blast area."

Terry snickers and shakes his head. "You think they'll just let us go? You think that if this *is* an experiment that they'll just let us drive through the perimeter back to our previous lives? No questions asked?"

"So what's your plan, doctor? Hmm? Same as before? Just sit on that stool until you starve to death? This is your fault, so if you have the solution we're all fucking ears."

My words hang heavy in the air, the group paralyzed by the tension.

Stella finally interjects. "I think you're right, Dominic?"

"What?" Terry asks, incredulous.

"He's right, Terry, we have to leave at some point. We have to try. Maybe this *was* a mistake after all. Maybe we were supposed to be part of some experiment and it all went badly. Spread out of control like a forest fire. That's possible, right?"

"You just said yourself they don't make mistakes like this. Are you now saying the opposite?"

"I don't know! I just know we're going to die if we stay!"

Terry stares back down at the bar, as if studying the cracks of the countertop. "I'm driving."

Stella smiles and looks at me.

"The hell you are," I reply.

CHAPTER FIVE

THE ENGINE OF THE REFRIGERATED truck grumbles in protest on the first attempt at ignition, but on the second attempt, it takes the bait, and we all sense the communal sigh of relief at the satisfying sound of the crankshaft rumbling to life.

The snow hasn't fallen for four days now, and the temperature is lingering just below freezing; but the sun is shining bright in the clear sky, and the snow that has piled high gives little resistance to the eight-ton truck.

"Are they following?" Terry asks from the back of the truck. He's decided to separate himself from the rest of us in a what appears to be a pout of some kind. Tom and Stella have squeezed between Danielle and I on the long front bench seat, and James occupies the jerry-rigged captain's seat just behind us.

"No, they're just standing there," Stella says. "I've always felt they were afraid of cars and trucks. I don't think they like the sound."

"Well if they get too close," I say, "they're going to like a whole lot less than that."

After a half hour of driving and only fifteen miles, Terry makes a request from his protest position in the back. "I need to stop."

I ignore him, and then he repeats himself. "Dominic, I need to stop."

"For what?"

"What do you think?"

"Are you serious?"

"It's not something I can help."

I look over at Stella and she nods, confirming the validity of Terry's urgency. I have no desire for more details.

"I saw a sign for a gas a few miles back. It should be coming up."

"A gas station? We're not on a family trip to Niagara Falls. Dig a hole in the snow and get to it."

The entire truck is quiet, and I can feel the eyes on me, judging my lack of compassion.

"Might as well keep life as normal as we can," Tom says, the old-guy wisdom dripping from his voice. "That sign said a BP should be right here at this exit."

"Yeah, I saw it." I glance in the rearview. "You really can't wait another thirty minutes?"

"I can barely wait another three."

To this point, the interstate has been slow but passable, and it appears that even a car or two has traversed it at some point during the last few days. We're cautious about building hope, and we take the evidence for what it is: a sign of other survivors.

But for all the allowances offered by the main road, the exit ramp forbids. It's a rising ramp, a c-shaped road that circles up to a high ground upon which the lone service station sits. I regret veering onto the ramp just a moment too late, just a second before I can straighten the truck back toward the interstate.

At the beginning of the bend in the exit, the truck's right tire slips from the road and slides forward, ignoring the commands of the steering wheel, and sticks into a large snow bank.

"Dammit!" I slam the gear shift into reverse but get only spin, and then shift to park and immediately hop from the truck to assess the crisis. It doesn't appear fatal. By the looks of the situation, we can wedge one of the pallets from the back of the truck under the wheel and give ourselves some leverage to reverse back. We might need some bodies to give it a push, but we have gravity on our side.

"Hey doctor!" I yell, kneeling in front of the truck. "Your potty stop has been rescinded. The snow is now your friend."

"He's walking." James has made his way to the front of the truck to check on my progress. I can see him staring off up the ramp. "Looks like he's committed to that station."

"What the hell?"

I stand and watch with James as Terry comically slogs through two feet of heavy, melting snow, marching like some Russian deserter toward the BP station.

"Thought he couldn't hold it. It's gonna take him fifteen minutes to get up there." I cup my hands around my nose and mouth. "Hey doctor! We need some help down here. I need you to help push this truck back."

The doctor keeps marching, either not hearing me or pretending not to.

"Do you think we can get it free?" Danielle has arrived and lines up with James and me to watch Terry trudge ahead.

"I think so," I reply. "We'll need to clear one of the palates. Might need to break it into pieces and use one of the slats. I'll need a hammer from the toolbox. Maybe the rubber mallet."

"What are we going to do about him?"

I turn to Danielle. "I'm going to follow him."

TERRY STOPS SUDDENLY just before reaching the top of the exit and stands as straight as a silo, staring. It's as if he is suddenly caught in the tractor beam of an alien spaceship. His last steps were desperate and exhausted, allowing me to close the gap on him. I'm only fifty yards or so back, maybe less. I am depleted myself, my feet like magnets to the snow around them. But I keeping moving, now convinced of my suspicions about the doctor and his dedication to reaching the station.

And then I see the source of his fixation. It's no spaceship, but its presence is no less startling.

First to appear is the muzzle and barrel, piercing the horizon as if born from the ether. And then the rest of the tank follows, tracks and wheels crushing the white snow below like talc, turret rising high and bulky, a menacing ornament atop a metallic mountain of death.

I stop and assume the same posture as Terry, frozen by the surreality in front of me. But unlike Terry, my paralysis lasts only a moment. My instincts kick on to flight mode, and I turn back toward the interstate. I was correct to be wary of the doctor, but the clichéd cautions of curiosity have proven correct once again.

I plot my tracks back to the truck, mapping out the snowprints we both left on the ascension, and start down the ramp, hopping comically in and out of the deep white holes.

"I have the data, Colonel," I hear from behind me. It's Terry, his voice is at once raving and fearful. "Everything. They *are* prone to violence. Not at first, not when they first noticed us, but as time went on they became aggressive. Murderous."

Unable to resist the temptation, I turn back toward the tank to see that a man has now appeared on the landscape, his body tall and rigid, head directly below the barrel. From my perspective, he looks as if he's just arrived from Central Casting. Salt-and-pepper hair, chiseled chin, full military regalia. He's flanked on either side by equally imposing soldiers, M16s gripped and ready.

"You're three weeks early, doctor," he booms. "Ten weeks. That was the experiment." I've no doubt he's chosen his volume so that I can hear him loud and clear.

"But I have what you asked for," Terry replies, pleading. "I've studied them. At great risk. I've carried out my role in the mission. It's as we believed. They can be weaponized." There's a pause of deafening silence, and then "I'm coming with you!"

"You were to arrive back here at ten weeks." The colonel's voice is calm but stern. "And alone. By my count, that's 0 for two, doctor."

Terry turns back and looks at me, and then pivots back to the colonel. "I had no choice. They insisted we leave. But...but I led them here. And I've brought the reports. We'll leave them. Keep them contained inside the perimeter. They'll never know what happened."

"No one's coming back. Not now. Not ever."

It's all I need to hear, and I again begin in earnest to make my way down the ramp, trying to build up momentum on my hopeless journey back to the truck.

"No!"

The doctor's scream triggers another burst of adrenaline, and I push with all my strength through the snow, using gravity to help propel me back down the exit. I wait for the soldiers' bullets to scream past me, but none come. "Start the truck!"

I can see that the group has almost managed to free the wheel from the bank, and as I get closer, I can hear the truck running. Another fifty feet and I'll have made it.

"Where have you been?" Stella calls. "Where is Ter—?"

I turn back to see what Stella's eyes have fixed on, but before it comes into view I hear it. The tank, in all its massiveness, rolling unstoppably down the exit ramp toward the truck. No need to say anything. It's time to go.

"Terry!" Stella yells, near tears.

"It was him." Is all I can manage, my exhaustion nearly complete as I reach the truck. I realize the words don't come close to explaining the dialogue I heard only moments before, but I pray there will be time for explanations later.

Tom, positioned in the driver's seat and seeming to understand on some basic level what is happening, pulls the gearshift to drive, foot on the brake. "Let's go, kids."

Stella and I squeeze into the passenger door and make our way back to the cargo. Tom and James are on the front bench.

Tom releases the brake and pushes the accelerator, but the back wheels spin impotently, whizzing in their nests of snow. It was too much gas, I think to myself. Gotta lay off a bit, Tom.

But the delay has just saved us. The stall has prevented us from driving head first into a crater left by the mortar that has just flown above us, landing thirty yards ahead with enormous destruction. Had the truck broken free, we would have caught the full force of the rocket with our lives.

The blast is deafening, stunning in its collateral power, but Tom stays calm, and I realize at that moment he's former military. Has to be.

"That's an old model," he says. "Gonna take a few seconds to reload. But I need this damn truck to get going."

Tom gives the accelerator pedal another punch, and on cue, the truck surges from the last of the embankment. From the rear of the bed we hear the cry of "Go!"

"Oh my god," Danielle whispers, staring into the side view mirror.

"Who was that?" Tom asks.

"It was Terry. I just saw him. He was behind us. He gave us the push we needed to clear the bank."

"We have to stop for him," Stella pleads, her voice is calm, but her eyes reveal the hysteria bubbling just beneath her surface.

I meet Tom's gaze in the rearview, and simply shake my head slowly. There's no redemption for Terry, other than the act he's just performed to save us. If we stop for him, we die.

Tom maneuvers the truck deftly past the crater and gets the truck up to speed on the interstate. "I'm sorry Stella." And then, "Hang on!" Tom turns the wheel slowly to the left without slowing, keeping the delicate balance between evasion on a slick road and flipping the truck on its side.

Blind to the actions behind us, Stella and I brace ourselves for impact, and feel the ground shake again as the mortar misses somewhere to the right of us.

Tom straightens the truck out again and resumes the path down the interstate. "We'll be well out of range before they can fire again. We should be safe now."

I LIVE TWENTY-EIGHT miles from Warren, and when we arrive at my house, it looks like an abandoned shell among many in the blast zone. I had little reason to expect otherwise, to believe my street was spared—after all, the group had told me of their explorations of at least fifty miles—but I had held out hope.

No more.

My street looks deserted at first glance, an abandoned ice planet, but as my eyes adjust to the landscape, I can see them peering from behind cars and hedges. Their black eyes now appearing malevolent in the context of what I know about them, of what I saw with Naia.

Tom pulls the truck into the driveway and parks it with the engine running. "I wouldn't carry any hope with you to that door, Dominic," he offers. "Can't be anything good inside."

"No, Tom, I don't expect there is."

"So what are we doing here?" Danielle asks. "Let's keep driving until we reach somewhere civilized, until we find the edge of this insanity."

I step out of the passenger door and stand on the snow-covered pavement, staring back into the faces of my new friends. From the corner of my eye, just at the edge of my periphery, I see a movement inside my house, a white flash in the dining room and then it's gone. Nobody in the truck sees it.

"We'll wait here for you, son," Tom says. His tone is matter-of-fact, as if his statement goes without saying.

"Tom. And the rest of you," I reply. My face is somber, my look piercing, serious. "You're leaving. You're going to find out what happened here, in this county, in this state, however far it goes." I look at Stella. "I've told you everything I know, everything I heard on that ramp. What Terry and the colonel said. Use it. Blackmail people if you have to. Find some media that still exists and broadcast the story everywhere."

"We're not leaving you, Dominic." It's Danielle, and she is clearly not open to discussion. "So do what you have to, but we'll be right here."

I look at James and then back to Tom, both of whom hold the same posture as Danielle. Stella is more stoical. I lock on Tom. "I want you to go when...if things go badly." I want to say more, leave them with profound words of parting, but all I can say is, "Thank you all for getting me here."

I follow the L-shaped sidewalk that leads from my driveway and climb the three small steps to my front door. I see the figure again at the dining room window, this time crouched and watching, peering at me over the sill. My wife. She probably danced in the snow when it started to fall, admiring the beauty, just as she tried to do with everything.

I fish the key from beneath the planter and unlock the door. I hear a shuffle inside; from behind me, I hear the scream of 'No!' They saw it this time, probably when it stood tall at the window, preparing to greet me the second I walk through the door, just as the three Thai restaurant owners greeted Naia.

But this is how it will be. This decision—to see my wife again—was made on that first day.

The knob catches a bit, just as it always did in my previous life, but I adjust the turn of my wrist and push in the door. She's standing in the foyer, a white shadow of the woman I used to love. I smile and feel a tear fall down my cheek as I close the door softly behind me, muffling the approaching screams of my fellow survivors.

DEAR READER,

I hope you enjoyed They Came with the Snow. They Came with the Snow was first released as a standalone novelette on March 22, 2017. Soon after publication, I began to hear from readers asking for more and wanting to know if I was planning on releasing part two of the story.

On July 23, 2018, I released The Melting, part two of the story. The Melting is much longer—about 235 pages.

In The Melting, the quest is no longer just to survive, it's to escape. The snow is melting, and the crabs are growing more violent.

At the base of a blocked-off bridge spanning the South River, Dominic and his friends plan a daunting journey to flee Warren County and the monsters that came when the snow fell.

But the crabs aren't the only danger they face.

There are other forces at work, forces with a secret as inhuman and terrifying as the crabs themselves.

And these forces are determined to never let the group leave.

Don't miss THE MELTING.

THE LIST, part three of the series, is also now available.

If you enjoyed They Came with the Snow, I'd be grateful if you left a review for it on Amazon. Your review doesn't have to be long. A simple, "I liked it!" is enough. That is, if you did like it, which I hope you did!

To stay in touch with me, visit my website:

CHRISTOPHERCOLEMANAUTHOR.COM

OTHER BOOKS BY CHRISTOPHER COLEMAN
THE SIGHTING SERIES
The Sighting (The Sighting Book One)
The Origin (The Sighting Book Two)
THE GRETEL SERIES
Gretel (Gretel Book One)
Marlene's Revenge (Gretel Book Two)
Hansel (Gretel Book Three)
Anika Rising (Gretel Book Four)
The Crippling (Gretel Book Five)

9 781793 056900